First published 1995 by Walker Books Ltd
87 Vauxhall Walk
London SE11 5HJ

Text © year of publication individual authors
Illustrations © year of publication individual illustrators
Main cover illustration © 1995 Helen Oxenbury

4 6 8 10 9 7 5 3

This book has been typeset in ITC Garamond.

Printed in Italy

British Library Cataloguing in Publication Data
A catalogue record for this book is available from the British Library.

ISBN 0-7445-4419-X

THE
WALKER
BOOK OF
BEDTIME
STORIES

WALKER BOOKS
AND SUBSIDIARIES
LONDON • BOSTON • SYDNEY

CONTENTS

HORATIO'S BED

All night Horatio could not sleep.
He tossed and turned, and
wriggled, and rolled. But he
just could not get comfortable.
I'll go and ask James what's
the matter, he thought.

James was busy drawing. Horatio sat down.
"I couldn't sleep all night," he said.
"Is it your bed?" asked James.
"I haven't got a bed," Horatio said.
"Then let's make
you one,"
said James.

by Camilla Ashforth

James took a clean sheet of paper from his Useful Box and very carefully drew a bed for Horatio. It was a big square bed with a leg at each corner.

Then he took another sheet of paper and drew another bed for Horatio. This one was a big square bed with a leg at each corner too. Horatio was very excited. He took one of James's drawings and tried to fold it into a bed.

Then he climbed inside it and closed his eyes.

It wasn't very comfortable and when Horatio rolled over … **RRRIIIPPP!**

James looked up. "That bed looks too hard to sleep on," he said and carried on with his drawing.

Horatio thought for a moment.

Then he pulled some feathers out of James's pillow and made a big square bed with them. But when he lay on it the feathers tickled his nose.

AAACHOO!
AAACHOO!
AAACHOO!

He sneezed and sneezed. James put down his pencil and blew away the feathers.

James sat Horatio down on his Useful Box.

"You wait here a minute," he said, "while I just finish drawing your bed." He had already drawn five square beds and was getting rather good at them.

But when James turned away, Horatio slipped down from the Useful Box. He wanted to see what James kept inside. He made some steps up to the lid. He pushed it open and leaned in. There were all sorts of things – buttons, brushes, keys and clothes pegs, clock wheels, clips and little bits of string.

Horatio looked for a bed. He couldn't find anything that looked like James's drawings. But he did find a big red sock. "Look, James!" he cried. "I've found your other sock!"

James did not seem very pleased. He didn't like anyone looking in his Useful Box. Not even Horatio.

Very quietly and carefully he started to put away his Useful Bits. When he had finished, he closed the lid and looked for Horatio. "Now we can make you a bed," he said.

But there was no need, because Horatio was fast asleep. His bed was not square and it did not have a leg at each corner.

But for little Horatio it was just right.

A Quiet Night In

by Jill Murphy

"I want you all in bed early tonight," said Mrs
Large. "It's Daddy's birthday and we're going to
have a quiet night in."

"Can we be there too?" asked Laura.

"No," said Mrs Large. "It wouldn't be quiet with you
lot all charging about like a herd of elephants."

"But we *are* a herd of elephants," said Lester.

"Smartypants," said Mrs Large. "Come on now,
coats on. It's time for school."

 That evening, Mrs Large had
the children bathed and in their
pyjamas before they had even
had their tea. They were all very cross.

"It's only half past four," said Lester. "It's not
even dark yet."

"It soon will be," said Mrs Large grimly.

 After tea, the children set about
making place cards and
decorations for the dinner table.
Then they all tidied up. Then Mrs Large tidied up again.

Mr Large arrived home looking very tired.

"We're all going to bed," said Lester.

"So you can be quiet," said Laura.

"Without us," said Luke.

"Shhhh," said the baby.

"Happy Birthday," said Mrs Large. "Come and see the table."

Mr Large sank heavily into the sofa. "It's lovely, dear," he said,
"but do you think we could have our dinner on trays in front of
the TV? I'm feeling a bit tired."

"Of course," said Mrs Large.

"It's *your* birthday. You can have whatever you want."

"We'll help," said Luke.

The children ran to the kitchen and brought two trays.

"I'll set them," said Mrs Large. "We don't want everything ending up on the floor."

"Can we have a story before we go to bed?" asked Luke.

"Please," said Lester.

"Go on, Dad," said Laura. "Just one."

"Story!" said the baby.

"Oh, all right," said Mr Large. "Just one, then."

Lester chose a book and they all cuddled up on the sofa.

Mr Large opened the book and began to read: "One day Binky Bus drove out of the big garage. 'Hello!' he called to his friend, Micky Milkfloat –"

"I don't like that one," said Laura. "It's a boy's story."

"Look," said Mr Large, "if you're going to argue about it, you can all go straight to bed without *any* story."

So they sat and listened while Mr Large read to them.

After a while he stopped.

"Go on, Daddy," said Luke. "What happened after he bumped into Danny Dustcart?"

"Did they have a fight?" asked Lester.

"Look," said Laura. "Daddy's asleep."

"Shhhh!" said the baby.

Mrs Large laughed. "Poor Daddy," she said.
"Never mind, we'll let him snooze a bit longer
while I take you all up to bed."
"Will you just finish the story, Mum?" asked Lester.
"We don't know what happens in the end," said Luke.
"Please," said Laura.
"Story!" said the baby.

"Move up, then," said Mrs Large.
She picked up the book and began to read:
"'Watch where you're going, you silly
Dustcart!' said Binky. Just then, Pip the
Police Car came driving by…"
After a while, Mrs Large stopped reading.

18

"What's that strange noise?" asked Lester.
"It's Mummy snoring," said Luke. "Daddy's snoring too."
"They must be very tired," said Laura, kindly.
"Shhhh!" said the baby.
The children crept from the sofa and fetched a blanket. They covered Mr and Mrs Large and tucked them in.

"We'd better put ourselves to bed," said Lester. "Come on."
"Shall we take the food up with us?" asked Luke. "It *is* on trays."
"It's a pity to waste it," said Laura. "I'm sure they wouldn't mind. Anyway, they wanted a quiet night in."
"Shhhh!" said the baby.

What Is the Sun?

by Reeve Lindbergh
illustrated by Stephen Lambert

What is the sun?
The sun is a star.

Is the sun near?
No, it is far.

What does it do?
It sends light down to you.

Like my lamp, only higher?
More like a big fire.

Can I see it at night?
No, you see the moonlight.

The moon is a star?
Not a star, just a place.

What else does it do?
It pulls the tides, too.

What are the tides?
The whole moving sea.

With the fish, and the whales?
Yes, definitely.

Why does it smile?
It looks like a face.

Where do tides go?
Up and down, ebb and flow.

Sometimes thin, sometimes fat?
Yes, the moon is like that.

On the beach where I play?
Up and down, night and day.

Does it shine in the day?
No, it just fades away.

Tides go out and go in?
Like your breath, and the wind.

What is the rain?
The rain makes things grow.

Like the flowers and trees?
And the rivers that flow.

Where does it rain?
On the sea, hill and plain.

And it rains on my head?
Not when you're here in bed!

And after the rain?
Then the earth's green again.

What is the wind?
Wind is air, blowing air.

Where does it blow?
Through the world, everywhere.

The wind comes and goes?
It goes right through your nose!

But that can be cold!
When deep winter takes hold.

Is wind ever warm?
In a summer rainstorm.

What is the earth?
It's our home – a big ball.

With the sun and the moon?
And the raindrops that fall.

And the wind and the tides?
And the people, besides.

Even children, like me?
Everybody you see.

So you'll be here too?
Yes, forever, with you.

Then I think it's all right.
I love you...Good night.

Good Night, Lily

by Martha Alexander

Read more, Lily. Lily sleepy.

Now Billy read. Look, Teddy.

Billy sleepy.

TOM AND PIPPO'S DAY

by Helen Oxenbury

When I wake up early in the morning, first I give Pippo a hug. Then we go to see if Mummy and Daddy are awake. Daddy has to hurry with his breakfast.

Sometimes I give
Pippo some of mine,
but he's so clumsy
and he makes a mess.

Pippo and I do things
together all day,
until Daddy
comes home.

When it's bedtime, I sometimes don't
know where Pippo is and I have to
look everywhere
until I find him.

Because when it's time
to go to sleep, I need
to be with Pippo.

THE WISH FACTORY
by Chris Riddell

Oliver used to have a
bad dream about a monster.
But one night a cloud came
instead of the dream …

and carried Oliver into the big, blue night –
far, far away to the Wish Factory.

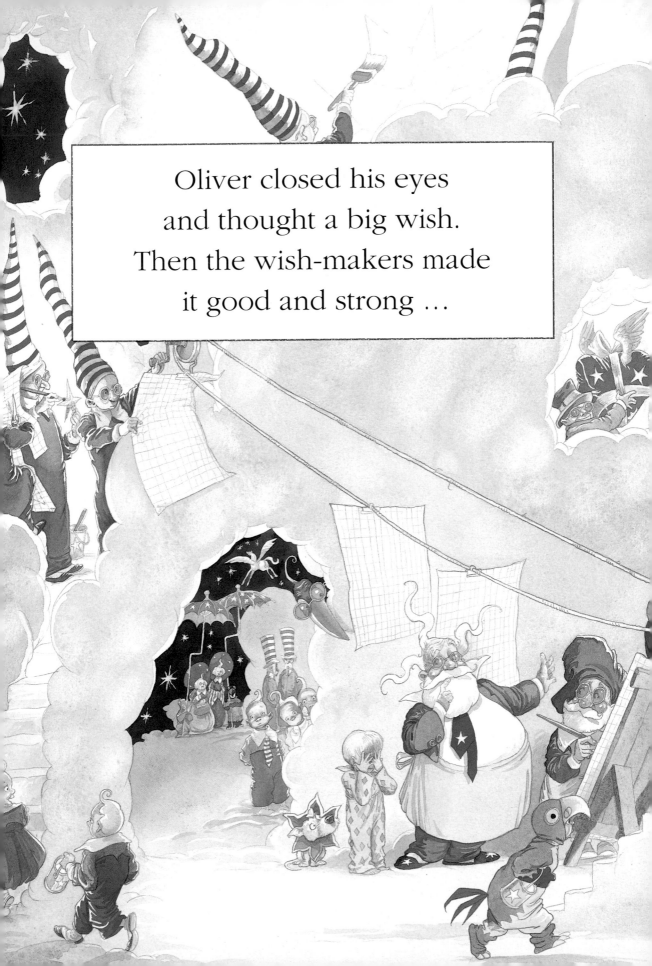

Oliver closed his eyes
and thought a big wish.
Then the wish-makers made
it good and strong …

and wrapped it up to keep it fresh.

"We hope it comes true," they said.

Then Oliver was in his own bed
and dreaming …

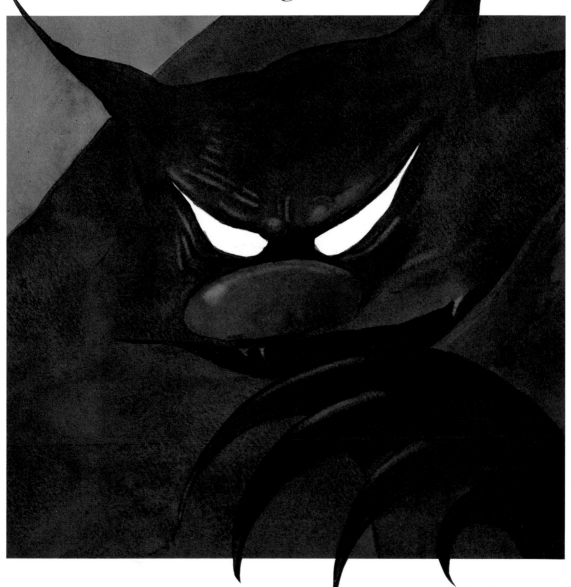

THE BIG BAD DREAM.

So Oliver untied the ribbon
and out came the wish …

and the wish came true.

The monster wasn't big any more,
and it wasn't bad. "BOO!" said Oliver.

And morning
came quite soon.

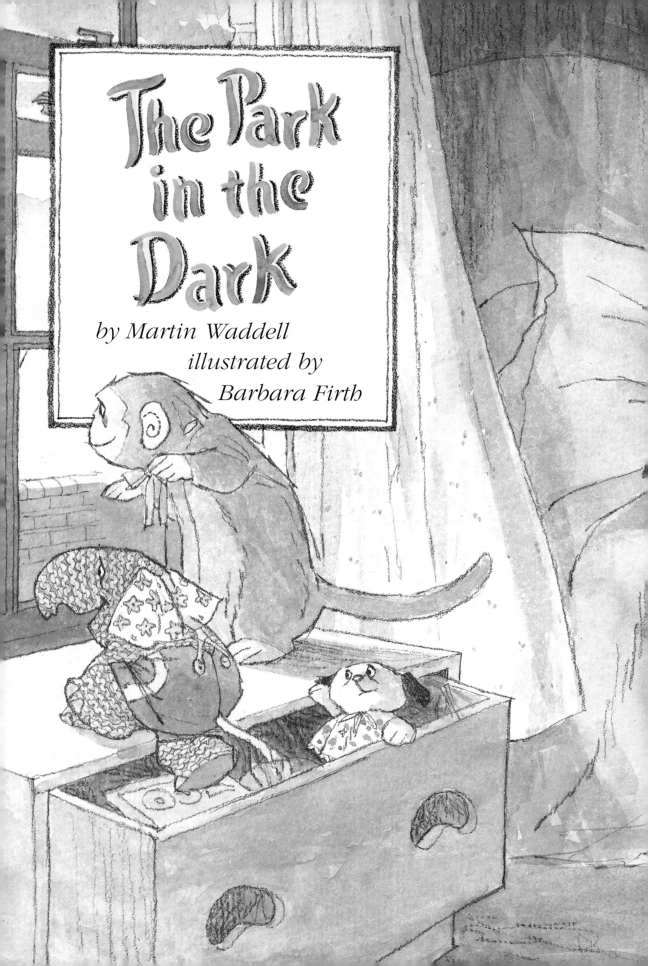

The Park in the Dark

by *Martin Waddell*

illustrated by

Barbara Firth

When the sun goes down
and the moon comes up
and the old swing creaks
in the dark,
that's when we go to the park,
    me and Loopy
        and Little Gee,
            all three.

Softly down the staircase,
through the haunty hall,
trying to look small,
    me and Loopy
        and Little Gee,
            we three.

It's shivery
out in the dark
on our way to the park,
down dustbin alley,
past the ruined mill,
so still,
    just me and Loopy
        and Little Gee,
            just three.

And Little Gee doesn't like it.
He's scared of the things he might see
in the park in the dark
with Loopy and me.
    That's me and Loopy
        and Little Gee,
            the three.

There might be moon witches
or man-eating trees
or withers that wobble
or old Scrawny Shins
or hairy hobgoblins,
or black boggarts' knees in the trees,
or things we can't see,
    me and Loopy
        and little Gee,
            all three.

But there's not, says Loopy,
and I agree,
and Little Gee gets up on my back
and we pass the Howl Tree,
    me and Loopy
        and Little Gee.
            We're heroes, we three.

In the park in the dark
by the lake and the bridge,
that's when we see
where we want to be,
    me and Loopy
        and Little Gee.
            WHOOPEE!

And we swing and we slide
and we dance and we jump
and we chase all over the place,
    me and Loopy
        and Little Gee,
            the Big Three!

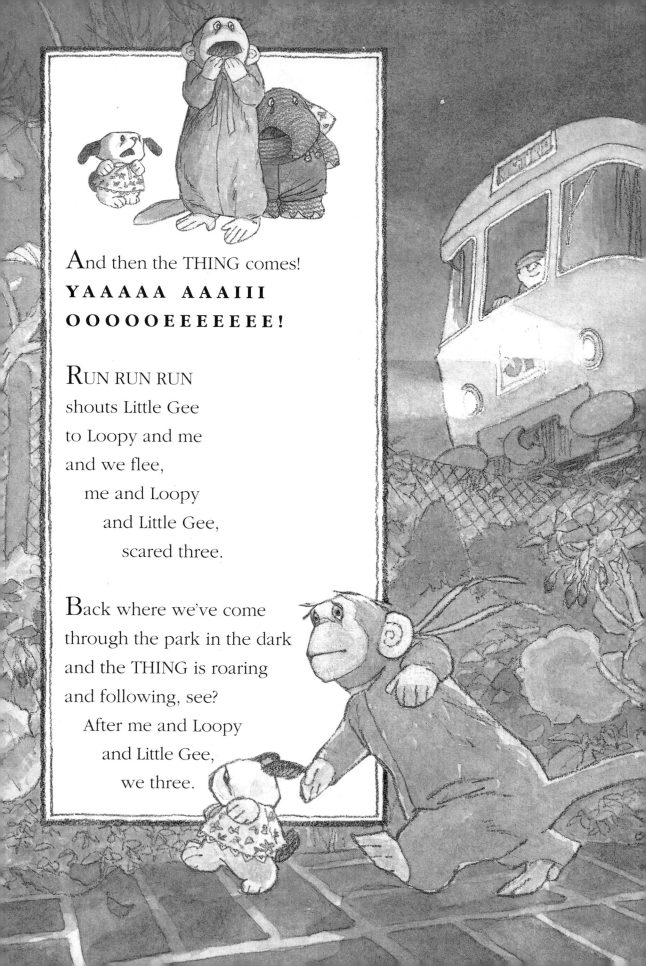

And then the THING comes!
**YAAAAA AAAIII
OOOOOEEEEEEE!**

RUN RUN RUN
shouts Little Gee
to Loopy and me
and we flee,
    me and Loopy
        and Little Gee,
            scared three.

Back where we've come
through the park in the dark
and the THING is roaring
and following, see?
    After me and Loopy
        and Little Gee,
            we three.

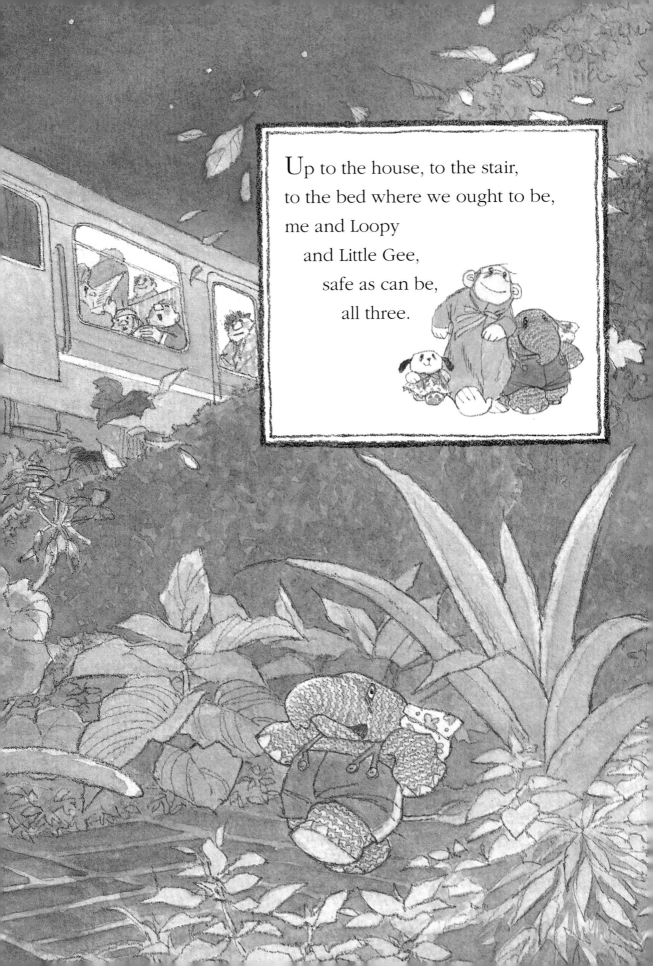

Up to the house, to the stair,
to the bed where we ought to be,
me and Loopy
and Little Gee,
safe as can be,
all three.

◆ TEN IN THE BED ◆
by Penny Dale

There were ten in the bed

and the little one said, "Roll over, roll over!"
So they all rolled over and Hedgehog fell out …

BUMP!

There were nine in the bed
and the little one said,
"Roll over, roll over!"
So they all rolled over
and Zebra fell out …

OUCH!

There were eight in the bed
and the little one said,
"Roll over, roll over!"
So they all rolled over
and Ted fell out …

THUMP!

There were seven in the bed
and the little one said,
"Roll over, roll over!"
So they all rolled over
and Croc fell out …

THUD!

There were four in the bed
and the little one said,
"Roll over, roll over!"
So they all rolled over
and Nellie fell out …

CRASH!

There were six in the bed
and the little one said,
"Roll over, roll over!"
So they all rolled over
and Rabbit fell out …

BONK!

There were three in the bed
and the little one said,
"Roll over, roll over!"
So they all rolled over
and Bear fell out …

SLAM!

There were five in the bed
and the little one said,
"Roll over, roll over!"
So they all rolled over
and Mouse fell out …

DINK!

There were two in the bed
and the little one said,
"Roll over, roll over!"
So they all rolled over
and Sheep fell out …

DONK!

There was one in the bed
and the little one said,
"I'm cold! I miss you!"

So they all came back and jumped into bed –
Hedgehog, Mouse, Nellie, Zebra, Ted, the little one, Rabbit, Croc,
Bear and Sheep.

Ten in the bed,
all fast asleep.

by Jan Ormerod

MIDNIGHT PILLOW FIGHT

Have *you* ever woken up in the middle of the night?
Have *you* ever had a midnight pillow fight?

Polly has ... and look how it started.

Polly thought her pillow was alive.
She thought it wanted to play.

Has *your* pillow ever wanted to
play in the middle of the night?

Polly's has.

Polly and her pillow went
downstairs on tiptoe.

Polly peeped and what did she see?
Some cushions were awake too.
For a moment Polly stood and watched.
I wonder what she felt, don't you?

This is how Polly said hello.
And this is how they played.

Now where did these big
cushions come from?

Have *you* ever marched
and danced like this …
having lots of fun in the
middle of the night?

Look, they played leapfrog.

Up and over …
up and over …
up and over!

BUMP! Pillow got squashed!
"Oh, poor pillow!"

And then the pillow fight began.

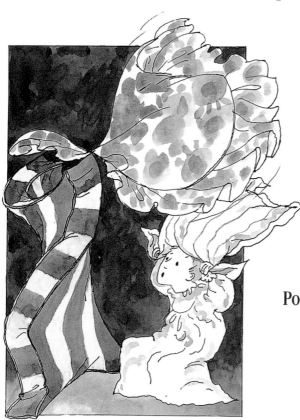

Ready, steady…

WHOOSH! WALLOP!

WHOOSH! WHOP!

WHOOSH! WHOP!

WALLOP!

"Please stop!"
Polly put on the light.

And the pillow
fight stopped.

Polly put the
cushions back in
their places.

Everything was
still again.

Polly took her
pillow up to bed.

Why do you
think she
looked so sad?

Have *you* ever hugged your pillow in the middle of the night? Polly has.
And look! All the cushions came upstairs to see if Polly was all right.

Have *you* ever
woken up in
the middle of
the night?

Have *you*
ever had a
midnight
pillow fight?

Polly has …
and this is
how it ended.

THIS IS THE BEAR AND THE SCARY NIGHT

by Sarah Hayes illustrated by Helen Craig

This is the boy
who forgot his bear
and left him behind
in the park on a chair.

Bye-bye!

This is the bear
who looked at the moon
and hoped the boy
would come back soon.

This is the bear
alone in the park.
These are the eyes which
glowed in the dark.

Wait for
me!

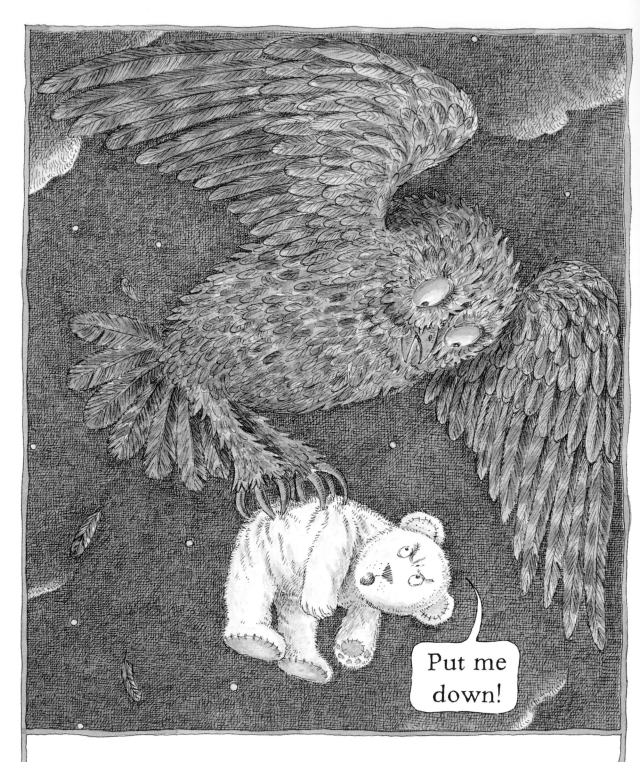

This is the owl
who swooped in the night
and gave the bear
a terrible fright.

This is the bear
up in the sky.
This is the owl
who struggled to fly.

These are the claws
which couldn't hold on.
And this is the bear who
fell … into … the pond.

This is the bear
who floated all night.
This is the dark which
turned into light.

This is the man
with the slide trombone
who rescued the bear
and took him home.

Out you
come.

This is the bear
in a warm blue sweater
who made a friend
and felt much better.

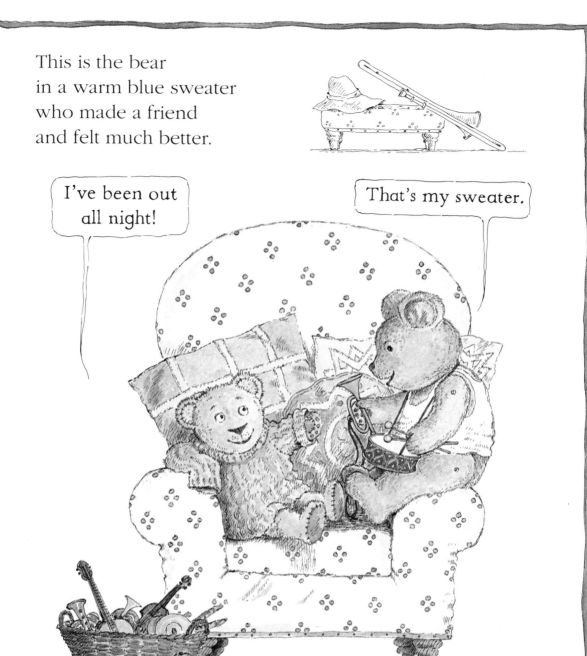

I've been out
all night!

That's my sweater.

This is the boy
who remembered his bear
and ran to the park
and found him there.

This is the bear
who started to tell
how he flew through the
air and how he fell . . .

and how he floated
and how he was saved
and how he was
terribly, terribly brave.

And this is the boy
who grinned and said,
"I know a bear
who is ready for bed."

Bounce Bounce Bounce

A Knee-ride Rhyme

by *Kathy Henderson*

illustrated by *Carol Thompson*

Chairs are for sitting on.
Bounce bounce bounce!

Beds are for lying on.
Dance dance dance!

Teddies are for cuddling.
Up in the air and down!

And clothes are for putting on.
Round and round and round!

Saucepans are for cooking in.
Crash crash crash!

Water is for washing with.
Splash splash splash!

Cots are for sleeping in.
Squeak squeak squeak!

And parents, what are parents for?
Sleep sleep sleep!

A BIG DAY FOR Little Jack

by Inga Moore

take to the party and some
new shoes for him to wear.
"Now we will buy you
a jacket," said Daddy. "You
must look smart if you are
going to a party."
Little Jack Rabbit had never
been to a party before. He
had never had to look smart.
"Will *you* come with me?"
he asked. "Will *you* come
to the party?"
"Daddies aren't invited,
Little Jack," said Daddy.

One day the postman brought
a card for Little Jack Rabbit.

Mummy read it out. It said,
"You are invited to a party."
Little Jack had never been to
a party before.
"Will you come with me?"
he asked.
"Mummies aren't invited,
Little Jack," said Mummy.

Little Jack Rabbit went
shopping with Daddy.
They bought a
present for
Little Jack to

At home Little Jack Rabbit's
sisters Nancy, Rhona and
Rita wrapped up the present
in some blue and white
striped paper. "Don't forget
to take it to the party, Little
Jack," said Nancy.

Little Jack Rabbit had never been to a party before. He had never had to look smart and he had never taken a present.
"Will *you* come with me?" he asked.
"Big sisters aren't invited, Little Jack," said Nancy.

Before the party Little Jack Rabbit's big brother Buck gave him a hot soapy bath. Buck had been to lots of parties.
"What are parties like?" asked Little Jack.
"You'll play party games," said Buck, "and make new friends."
Little Jack Rabbit had never been to a party before. He had never had to look smart and he had never taken a present. He had *never* played party games or made new friends.
"Will *you* come with me?" he asked.
"Big brothers aren't invited, Little Jack," said Buck.

Granpa had been mending a toy for Little Jack Rabbit. It was Little Jack's favourite toy, Bunnikin.
"Why aren't you ready, Little Jack?" Granpa asked. "You will be late for the party."
"I don't want to go," said Little Jack Rabbit.
"Why not?" asked Granpa.
"I don't want to go on my own," said Little Jack.
"Why don't you go with Bunnikin?" asked Granpa.
"Are Bunnikins invited?" asked Little Jack Rabbit.
"Oh, yes," said Granpa, "I should think so, Little Jack. I should think Bunnikins are invited."

So Little Jack Rabbit put on his smart new jacket and his shiny new shoes and he went to the party with Bunnikin.

Little Jack Rabbit held on to Bunnikin. He played

What's the Time, Mr Wolf? and *Pop Goes the Weasel!* But when he tried to play *Pass the Parcel* he had to leave Bunnikin on the ground – and when he came back, what did he find …

them together," said Rosy. "Come on, let's go and have some tea."

After tea Little Jack Rabbit had such fun playing with his new friend Rosy, he didn't want to go home when Granpa came to fetch him.

"Don't forget Bunnikin, Little Jack," said Granpa.

but a teddy sitting next to Bunnikin. The teddy belonged to Rosy.

"I've never been to a party before," said Rosy. "Is that why you brought Teddy?" asked Little Jack Rabbit. "Yes," said Rosy. "I brought Bunnikin," said Little Jack. "I think Teddy likes Bunnikin," said Rosy. "Bunnikin likes Teddy," said Little Jack. "Perhaps we should leave

It had been a big day for Little Jack Rabbit. He had been to his first party.

"I'm going to another party soon," said Little Jack.
"Oh," said Mummy.
"It's Rosy's party," said Little Jack.

"Can I come with you?" asked Mummy.
"No," said Little Jack.
"But I'm your mummy," said Mummy.
"Mummies aren't invited," said Little Jack Rabbit.
"Good night, Little Jack," said Mummy.

Can't You Sleep, Little Bear?

by Martin Waddell • illustrated by Barbara Firth

Once there were two bears. Big Bear and Little Bear. Big Bear is the big bear, and Little Bear is the little bear. They played all day in the bright sunlight. When night came, and the sun went down, Big Bear took Little Bear home to the Bear Cave.

Big Bear put Little Bear to bed in the dark part of the cave. "Go to sleep, Little Bear," he said. And Little Bear tried. Big Bear settled in the Bear Chair and read his Bear Book by the light of the fire. But Little Bear couldn't get to sleep.

"Can't you sleep, Little Bear?" asked Big Bear, putting down his Bear Book (which was just getting to the interesting part) and padding over to the bed. "I'm scared," said Little Bear. "Why are you scared, Little Bear?" asked Big Bear. "I don't like the dark," said Little Bear. "What dark?" said Big Bear. "The dark all around us," said Little Bear.

Big Bear looked, and he saw that the dark part of the cave was very dark, so he went to the Lantern Cupboard and took out the tiniest lantern that was there. Big Bear lit the tiniest lantern and put it near to Little Bear's bed. "There's a tiny light to stop you being scared, Little Bear," said Big Bear. "Thank you, Big Bear," said Little Bear, cuddling up in the glow. "Now go to sleep, Little Bear," said

Big Bear, and he padded back to the Bear Chair and settled down to read the Bear Book by the light of the fire.

Little Bear tried to go to sleep, but he couldn't.

"Can't you sleep, Little Bear?" yawned Big Bear, putting down his Bear Book (with just four pages to go to the interesting bit) and padding over to the bed. "I'm scared," said Little Bear. "Why are you scared, Little Bear?" asked Big Bear. "I don't like the dark," said Little Bear. "What dark?" asked Big Bear. "The dark all around us," said Little Bear.

"But I brought you a lantern!" said Big Bear. "Only a tiny-weeny one," said Little Bear. "And there's lots of dark!"

Big Bear looked, and he saw that Little Bear was quite right, there was still lots of dark. So Big Bear went to the Lantern Cupboard and took out a bigger lantern. Big Bear lit the lantern, and put it beside the other one.

"Now go to sleep, Little Bear," said Big Bear, and he padded back to the Bear Chair and settled down to read the Bear Book by the light of the fire.

Little Bear tried and tried to go to sleep, but he couldn't.

"Can't you sleep, Little Bear?" grunted Big Bear, putting down his Bear Book (with just three pages to go) and padding over to the bed.

"I'm scared," said Little Bear. "Why are you scared, Little Bear?" asked Big Bear. "I don't like the dark," said Little Bear. "What dark?" asked Big Bear. "The dark all around us," said Little Bear. "But I brought you two lanterns!" said Big Bear. "A tiny one and a bigger one!" "Not much bigger," said Little Bear. "And there's still lots of dark."

Big Bear thought about it, and then he went to the Lantern Cupboard and took out the Biggest Lantern of Them All, with two handles and a bit of chain. He hooked the lantern up above Little Bear's bed. "I've brought you the Biggest Lantern of Them All!" he told Little Bear. "That's to stop you being scared!" "Thank you, Big Bear," said Little Bear, curling up in the glow and watching the shadows dance.

"Now go to sleep, Little Bear," said Big Bear, and he padded back to the Bear Chair and settled down to read the Bear Book by the light of the fire.

Little Bear tried and tried and tried to go to sleep, but he couldn't.

"Can't you sleep, Little Bear?" groaned Big Bear, putting down his Bear Book (with just two pages to go) and padding over to the bed. "I'm scared," said Little Bear. "Why are you scared, Little Bear?" asked Big Bear. "I don't like the dark," said Little Bear. "What dark?" asked Big Bear. "The dark all around us," said Little Bear. "But I brought you the Biggest Lantern of Them All, and there isn't any dark left," said Big Bear. "Yes, there is!" said Little Bear. "There is, out there!" And he pointed out of the Bear Cave at the night.

Big Bear saw that Little Bear was right. Big Bear was very puzzled. All the lanterns in the world couldn't light up the dark outside. Big Bear thought about it for a long time, and then he said, "Come on, Little Bear." "Where are we going?" asked Little Bear. "Out!" said Big Bear. "Out into the darkness?" said Little Bear. "Yes!" said Big Bear. "But I'm scared of the dark!" said Little Bear. "No need to be!" said Big Bear, and he took Little Bear by the paw and led him out of the cave into the night and it was ... DARK!

"Ooooh! I'm scared," said Little Bear, cuddling up to Big Bear. Big Bear lifted Little Bear, and cuddled him, and said, "Look at the dark, Little Bear." And Little Bear looked. "I've brought you the moon, Little Bear," said Big Bear.

"The bright yellow moon, and all the twinkly stars."

But Little Bear didn't say anything, for he had gone to sleep, warm and safe in Big Bear's arms. Big Bear carried Little Bear back into the Bear Cave, fast asleep, and he settled down with Little Bear on one arm and the Bear Book on the other, cosy in the Bear Chair by the fire.

And Big Bear read the Bear Book right to ...

THE END

◇ TEN OUT OF BED ◇

 There were ten

by **Penny Dale**

out of bed ...

and the little one said, "Let's play!"
And Hedgehog said, "Let's play **TRAINS!**"

So they all played trains until Hedgehog fell asleep.

There were nine out of bed and the little one said, "Let's play!"
And Ted said, "Let's play **SEASIDES!**"

So nine played seasides until Ted fell asleep.

There were eight out of bed and the little one said, "Let's play!"
And Rabbit said, "Let's play **THEATRES!**"

So eight played theatres until Rabbit fell asleep.

There were seven out of bed and the little one said, "Let's play!"
And Bear said, "Let's play **PIRATES!**"

So seven played pirates until Bear fell asleep.

There were six out of bed and the little one said, "Let's play!"
And Sheep said, "Let's play **DANCING!**"

So six played dancing until Sheep fell asleep.

There were five out of bed and the little one said, "Let's play!"
And Croc said, "Let's play **GHOSTS!**"

So five played ghosts until Croc fell asleep.

There were four out of bed and the little one said, "Let's play!"
And Nellie said, "Let's play **FLYING!**"

So four
played
flying
until Nellie
fell asleep.

There were three out of bed and the little one said, "Let's play!"
And Zebra said, "Let's play **CAMPING!**"

So three
played
camping
until Zebra
fell asleep.

There were two out of bed and the little one said, "Let's play!"
And Mouse said, "Let's play **MONSTERS!**"

So two
played
Monsters
until Mouse
fell asleep.

There was one out of bed and the little one said,
"I'm sleepy now!"

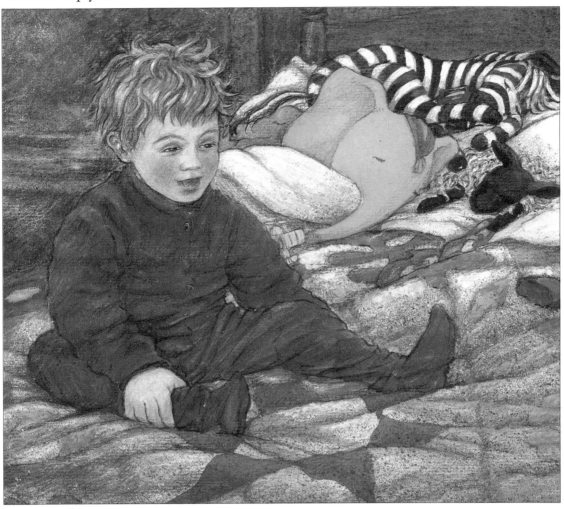

So he slipped under the covers next to Ted.
Good night, sweet dreams, ...ten in the bed.

When I'm BIG

by Debi Gliori

What are you doing up? It's way past your bedtime.

But I'm not sleepy.

Oh yes, you are. I'll tuck you in.

It's no fun being little... I wish I was big. One day I will be big and...

When I'm big, I'm going to stay up as late as I like and make myself marshmallows on toast instead of going to bed.

When I'm big, I'm going swimming with the whales in the deep blue sea instead of puddling about in the bath.

When I'm big, I'm going to wear a bird-suit and gumboots all day long instead of a jumper and dungarees.

When I'm big, I'm going to have a huge back garden with sand mountains that touch the sky and a lake in the middle instead of a sandpit and a paddling pool.

When I'm big, I'm going to drive the trolley round the shops with Dad in it instead of the other way round.

When I'm big, I'm going to grow triffids and Venus fly-traps and man-eating orchids instead of mustard and cress.

When I'm big, I'm going to ride a proper bike instead of a tricycle.

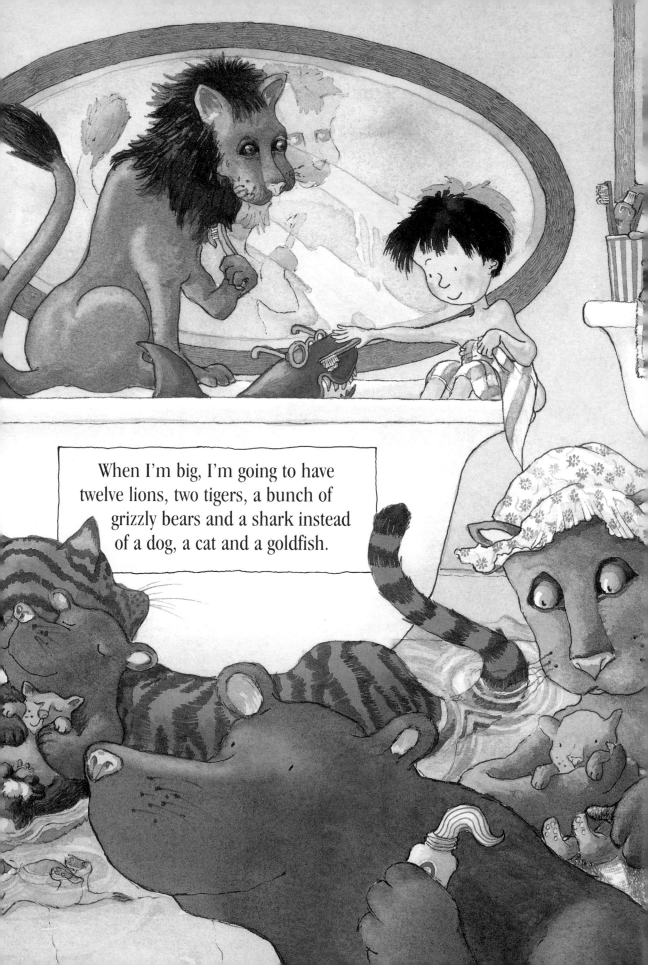

When I'm big, I'm going to have twelve lions, two tigers, a bunch of grizzly bears and a shark instead of a dog, a cat and a goldfish.

When I'm big, I'm going to put Mum and Dad to bed and read them a story and turn out the light and go downstairs on my own.

GET INTO BED!

by Virginia Miller

It was time for Bartholomew to go to bed.

"Ba, time for bed," George said.

"Nah!" said Bartholomew.

George said, "Brush your
teeth and go to bed."

"Nah!" said Bartholomew.

"Have you brushed your teeth yet, Ba?"

"Nah!" said Bartholomew,
beginning to cry.

"Come on, Ba,
into bed!"
George said.

"Nah!" said
Bartholomew.
"Nah, nah,
nah, nah,
NAH!" said
Bartholomew.

85

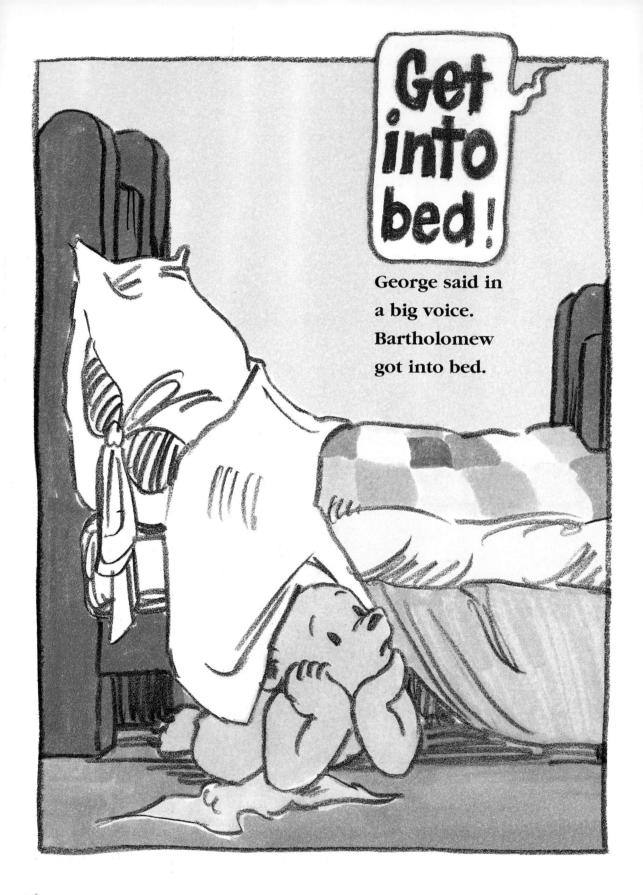

Get into bed!

George said in a big voice. Bartholomew got into bed.

He giggled
and wriggled,
he hid
and tiggled,
he cuddled
and huggled,
he snuggled
and sighed.

"Goodnight,
Bartholomew,"
said George.

said
Bartholomew
softly.

He gave a big
yawn, closed
his eyes and
went to sleep.

IN THE MIDDLE OF THE NIGHT

by Kathy Henderson
illustrated by Jennifer Eachus

A long time after bedtime
when it's very very late
when even dogs dream
and there's deep sleep
breathing through the house

when the doors are locked
and the curtains drawn
and the shops are dark
and the last train's gone
and there's no more traffic
   in the street
because everyone's asleep

then

the window-cleaner comes
to the high-street shop fronts
and shines at the glass
in the street-lit dark

and a dust-cart rumbles past
on its way to the dump

loaded with the last
of the old day's rubbish.

On the twentieth floor
of the office-block
there's a lighted window
and high up there
another night cleaner's
vacuuming the floor
working nights on her own
while her children sleep at home.

89

And down in the dome of the
   observatory
the astronomer who's waited all day
   for the dark
is watching the good black sky at last

for stars and moons
and spikes of light
through her telescope
in the middle of the night
while everybody sleeps.

and out by the gate
rows of parked vans wait
for their drivers to come
and take the newly-baked
bread to the shops
for the time when the
bread-eaters wake.

Across the town at the hospital
where the nurses watch in the
 dim-lit wards
someone very old shuts their eyes
and dies
breathes their very last breath
on their very last night.

At the bakery
the bakers in their floury clothes
mix dough in machines
for tomorrow's loaves of bread

Yet not far away on another floor

after months of waiting

a new baby's born

and the mother and the father

hold the baby and smile

and the baby looks up

and the world's just begun

but still everybody sleeps.

Now through the silent station

past the empty shops

and the office-blocks

past the sleeping streets

and the hospital

a train with no windows

goes rattling by

and inside the train the sorters sift

urgent letters and packets on the

late-night shift

so tomorrow's post will arrive in time

at the towns and the villages

down the line.

And the mother

with the wakeful child in her arms

walking up and down

and up and down

and up and down

the room

hears the train as it passes by

and the cats by the bins

and the night owl's flight

and hums hushabye and hushabye

we should be asleep now

you and I

it's late and time to close your eyes

it's the middle of the night.